MEL BAY PRESENTS

Café ACCORDION

BY DAN NEWTON

Transcribed by Gary Dahl

CD Contents

1	Say I Do [3:41]	9	Laura's Wedding [4:37]
2	April Waltz [2:45]	10	Café Accordion [5:0]
3	Eiffel Tower [5:15]	11	Telephone Polka [3:41]
4	Two French Waltzes [6:32]	12	Che Lia Lia [3:41]
5	Valiakainen-Merimes [3:54]	13	Musette [3:41]
6	Spanish Jenny [2:49]	14	Halloween [3:41]
7	Dust Bunnies [3:44]	15	Nuevo Brazil [3:41]
8	Election Rag [2:50]	16	Say I Do [3:41]

1 2 3 4 5 6 7 8 9 0

Contents

Foreword

When I set about to record a dozen or two of my favorite original and obscure old tunes that I performed frequently, I thought 50 cassettes or so would be the extent of the project. This gives you a clue to my sense of business and marketability. Good reviews in a number of music magazines, reprintings, pressing as a CD, being picked up by NPR's "All Things Considered", and now, a generous offer to be a Mel Bay Publications book! All I can say is I'm glad so many of you like the tunes, and I'm encouraged that the simple arrangements and production values of my project came across in an effective and pleasing way. I hope you will enjoy playing my tunes as much as I do, and pass them on to your friends.

Thanks.
Dan "Daddy Squeeze" Newton

Performance Notes

1. *Say I Do.* This was written for a wedding, as the title suggests. I wanted to create something simple and pretty, reflective and slightly bittersweet. It should be played to de-emphasize the "oom-pah-pah" in the bass hand. You can do this by holding the bass note through the first of the two following corresponding chords. This technique smooths out the sound of the accompaniment, as does the use of a drone from the bass button while shifting the chord button one measure at a time.

2. *April Waltz.* Another obvious title, this tune was written while watching an April shower knock the early blossoms off the trees. It was one of my earlier attempts at writing a musette style tune. The approach should be light. Note the form AA/BB/AA/CC/BB/A(variant)A. The A variant simply changes the octave of each of the first four measures of melody, and inverts the long glissando.

3. *Eiffel Tower.* I made this tune up the night before I went into the studio to record *Café Accordion.* I felt like I needed a tune or two with a different rhythm than most of the others. I really had decided not to try it but Leo, the engineer, encouraged me, and I hit it on the first try. The chord changes are based loosely on "Getting Sentimental Over You." For some reason, it seems like most of the guitarists I work with really like playing these changes. When I switch from F to E in the first line, I cheat and use the counter of C in the left hand for the bass note.

4. *Two French Valses.* I learned the first of these off a tape of French folk bands from the late 70s. The folkdance teacher who gave it to me labeled it just "valse." It is a nice example of where French folk music begins to cross over into musette. The second tune I picked up at sessions at the Lark In The Morning music camp near Mendocino. It has lyrics and a title, but I haven't been able to locate them. I have greatly exaggerated the ritard in the second section, and added an ending that should be traditionally used only for bourees. This was a popular Parisian song in the 1920s, I believe.

5. *Valiekeinen/Merimes.* Two more tunes from another tape given me by a folkdance instructor. These are both Finnish numbers, very well known in their homeland. "Valiekeinen" is a scottische (or yenkka, in Finnish) and probably shouldn't speed up in the 3rd part when played for dances. When I performed for 3 weeks in Finland, everybody sang along. I asked someone what the words meant—here is a rough translation: "Everything is temporary...the wine you drink...the food you eat...the songs you sing...and the money you spend for the love of a beautiful girl...and so is her love temporary...but also the sorrow you feel at the loss of her love, is temporary." "Merimes" is a sailors' dance, and very typical of Finnish polka music.

6. *Spanish Jenny.* This was my first attempt at writing something that most American gringos would call "Latin music." I was inspired by sounds I heard on tapes of Brazilian accordion music, specifically the style called Forro (pron. fo-hoh'). I named it because one section reminds me of a line in a song I heard on the radio a lot while I was growing up, about someone named Cotton Jenny. The improv or variation is mostly arpeggios, chromatic runs and little bluesy licks.

7. *Dust Bunnies.* I made this up while cleaning an apartment I was moving out of after 7 years. The first part is reminiscent of Fats Wallers' "Jitterbug Waltz," the second is kind of a hambo bit, and the third is an expansion of a theme found in the intro of a musette tune. All these influences prompted one local radio announcer to introduce this as my "plagiarism" waltz.

8. *Election Rag.* Not to be confused with an older piece "Election Day Rag" though it was composed while watching election returns. It's the only rag I've tried to make up. I don't play it very often, and it still gives me a few problems. Make sure you don't play it too fast.

9. *Laura's Wedding.* Like "Say I Do," written for a wedding, this time my own. It should also downplay the "oom-pah-pah" in the left hand. If I have a good accompanist, I usually leave out the left hand all together, except at the end. There, I have switched off the lower reeds on the bass, used the bass button as a drone while shifting the chords. This gives it a bit of a pump-organ or harmonium-like quality.

10. *Café Accordion.* The title was suggested by Jim Dryden, who did the beautiful cover art. Again, it's a tough one, still, for me to play. Just break it down into little sections and memorize finger patterns. Give the left hand a real light touch, too.

11. *Telephone Polka.* An Italian tune I picked up from Michael Hubbard at Lark in the Morning. He learned it from a mandolinist from Italy. I think he said it's also called the "Indian Polka." It's beautiful, and not too hard to play. People always seem to pick up on the fact that it's Italian right away.

12. *Musette.* This was my first attempt at writing something that sounded like French Musette. It's not necessary to play 3 against 2 the second time around like I do on the recording, but this is a nice rhythmic variation that does not require changing the melody. Even though it gives the tune a jig-like feel, it remains danceable.

13. *Halloween.* This tune has the feel of the "valse-java," a very popular form of musette that is closer to the Auvergnat origins of the music. I have added a third part that is slightly more swingy. I like to switch reeds to a brighter setting for that part. The syncopated feel is attained on the right hand, while keeping the left hand steady in 3/4 time.

14. *Nuevo Brazil.* Another tune inspired by the Forro accordion music of Brazil. The bass line is played tonic-chord-counter-alternate (C-chord-E-G). The improvisation in the middle on the recording is based on adding dominant 7 and 9 tones to the scales of B flat and C. I have a terrible bellows shake technique, so I simulate it by bouncing my finger tips on the keys, holding my fingers in contact with the keys while shaking from the wrist. This way I can get that shake effect on the melody side while keeping the bass tones fairly steady.

SAY I DO

B
G
M
D/F♯
M
D
G
M
Bm
Em
A
M
1.
D.C.
2.
D
M

APRIL MUSETTE (WALTZ)

If Needed (Ie. A/B/A/C/B/A).

* This Melody and These Chords. Add Bass if Needed.

2. to B
4. to Trio
6.
F
F
Fine
M
M
B
B♭
F7
M
7
B♭
M
B♭7
E♭
7
M

Eb Ebm Bb G7 C7 F7 Bb
D.C.
7
M
C Trio
Eb Bb7
M
7
Eb° Eb Gm Cm D7
d
M
7
1. 2.
Gm Bb Bb7 F to B
M 7

This page has been left blank to avoid awkward page turns

EIFFEL TOWER

D7+5
Gm9
G7-9
Csus
C
F
D7+5
D7
B♭m
F
Dm
Gm
C7
F
Dm
B♭m
C7
F

TWO FRENCH WALTZES

Valse in A minor

Traditional

2.
Am
B
Am
D
M
G
M
1.
Am
2.
Am
C
Am
G
M
C
M
F
C
G
M
1.
Am
2.
Am
D.S.
3.
Am
rit.

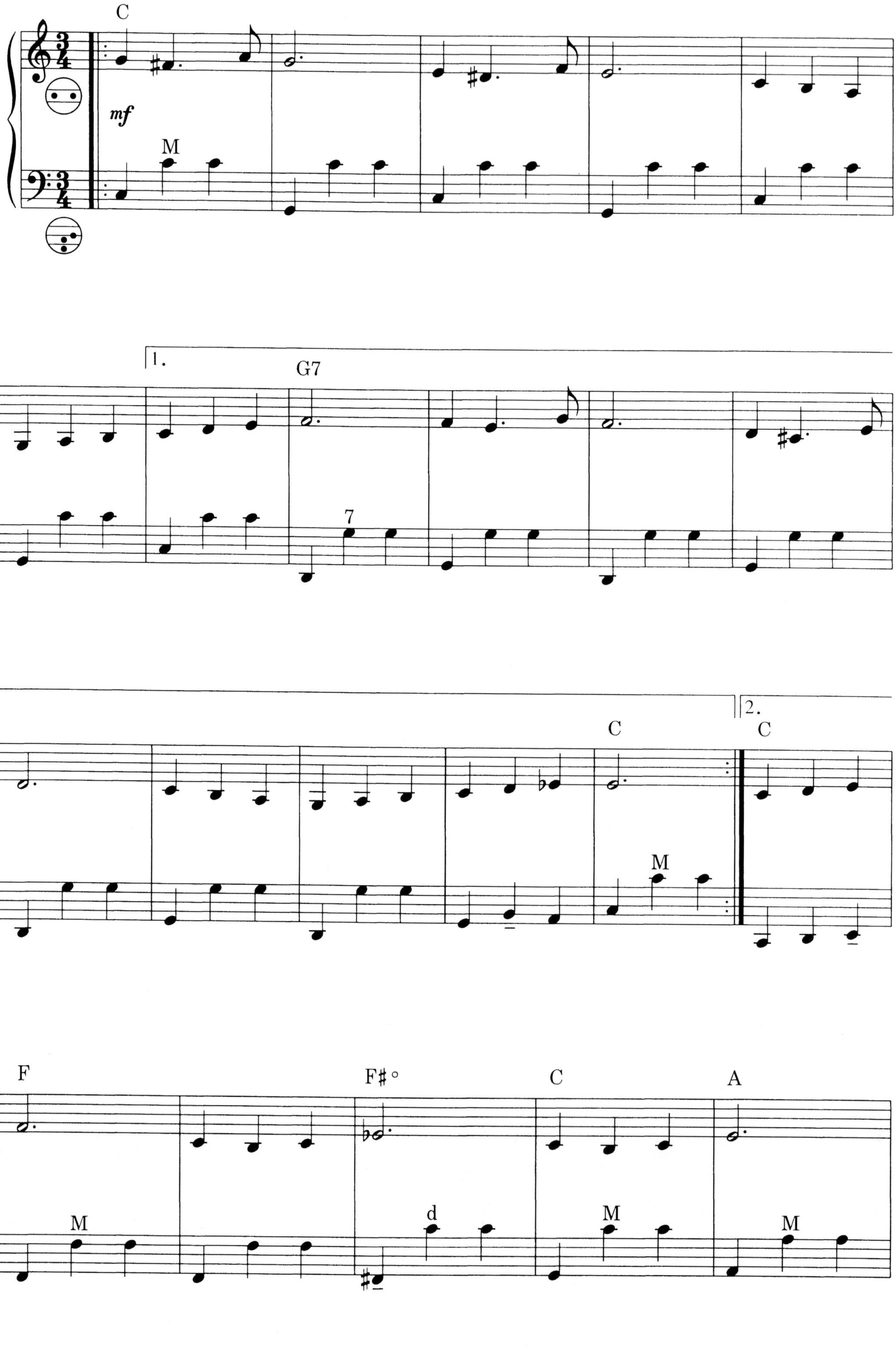
C
mf
M
1.
G7
7
2.
C
M
F
F♯○
d
C
M
A
M

D7
G
C
rit.
7
M
G
C
M
G
M
1.
2.
C
M

VALIEKEINEN / MERIMES

Traditional

2.
Dm
Gm
D7
7
C
Gm
accel.
Dm
A7
7
Dm
D7
Allegro
Gm
Dm
A7
7
1.
Dm
D7
7
2.
Dm
Gm
Dm
A
Merimes:
Dm
Gm
A
M
Dm
A
M
Dm
Gm
A
M
1.
Dm Gm Dm

2.
Dm Gm Dm C
B F
C7
M
7
1.
F C
2.
F A7
C Dm
Gm
A7
Dm
Gm
A7
Dm
D F
C7
F C7

F
C7
M
7
F
B♭
C7
M
M
7
F
C
F
B♭
M
M
M
M
C7
1.
F
C7
2.
D.S. al Φ
Φ
Dm
Fine
M
7
7
M

SPANISH JENNY

2.
Dm
C7
F
7
M
B
F
C
C♯°
Dm
M
d
A7
1.
B♭
F
7
M
M
G
A7
2.
Gm
M
7
F
A
1.
D
to C
2.
D
to D
M
M
M

D
M
A
A7
M
7
1.
2.
Dm
A7
7
Dm
A7
Dm
A7
to A
D
7
Gm
F
M
A7
7
1.
2.
D
M
D

DUST BUNNIES

Em
C7
F
7
M
A
Dm
Gm
C7
M
7
F
Dm
Gm
C7
F
1.
M
7
M
B
Dm
Gm
A7
Dm
7

Gm
A
M
Dm
Gm
A
M
3
Dm
Gm
A
M
3
D
M
G7
C7
7
7
C
F
M

E
Dm
Am
M
A7
Dm
B7
7
7
Em
Gm
C7
F
E
7
M
M
Dm
Am
A♭
C
Am
Fm
G7
C
C7
al Coda
M
7
M
7

ELECTION RAG

B
C
C7
F
Fm
B7
Em
G7
Am
D7
1.
to B
2.
D.S. al
(8va)
G
C
D
M
7

G G7 C F D
M M M M 7
G G7 F♯ Bm A7 D
M 7 M 7 M 7
G G7 C F B♭
M 7 M M M
E♭ A7 D7 G D.S. al ⊕⊕
7 7 M
⊕⊕ (8va) G
M 7
TAG C C♯° G E7 A7 G D7 G
M d M 7 7 7

LAURA'S WEDDING WALTZ

Gm C F C F B♭
M M
F C F C7 Dm
1. 2.
M M M 7
C Dm C F Gm Dm
M M
C Am Dm C F B♭
M M
F C Dm F F
1. 2. 3.
D.S.
M M M M

CAFE ACCORDION

A7
D7
Gm
Cm
E♭
1.
D7
2.
D7
B
Gm
Cm
D7
Gm
G7
C7
F

1.
2.
C
B♭
D7
Gm
G
G/F♯
G/E
G/D
G6
G♯ ◦
Am7
E7
Am
D7
Cm6
G7
M
7
d

Dm Fm Cmaj C6
Cm7 Cm6 G G/F♯ G/E
G/D Am D7
1.
G Em Am7 D7sus4
2. 3.
Gm
Cm Eb
1.
D7
to A
3.
D
rit.
M
7

TELEPHONE POLKA

Allegretto

Italian Traditional

C
E
A
E7
A
E7
D
A
E7
1.
A
to A
2.
A
M
7

MUSETTE

D7
G
D
7
A7
D
1.
2.
D7
B7
M
F♯7
Bm
E7
A7
F♯7
Bm
A7
1.
D
Bm
2.
D
A7
D.C.
3.
D

HALLOWEEN

B
D7
D7/F♯
Gm
Gm/B♭
D7/A
D7
Gm
G7
Cm
Gm
A7
D7
Gm
1.
2.
Gm/F♯
C7+5

C
F
G7
C
Dm
M
7
M
G7/B
C6
C/E
E♭
Dm
7
M
Fm
Em
Am
Dm
G
C
1.
B♭
to C
2.
D7
to A
3.
C
M
M
M
7
M

NUEVO BRAZIL

C
B G
C
G7
C G7
C7
F
M
C
B♭
3
M

C
1.
2.
A7
D7
G7
1. 2.
C
3.
C
M
M
A7
D7
G7
C
1. to A
2. to
B♭
G/B
C